W9-BEU-817

Participemos / Doing Our Part

Stephen es un buen nieto
Stephen Is a Good Grandson

Martin Gregory

traducido por / translated by Eida de la Vega

ilustrado por / illustrated by
Aurora Aguilera

PowerKiDS
press.

New York

Published in 2019 by The Rosen Publishing Group, Inc.
29 East 21st Street, New York, NY 10010

First Edition

Translator: Eida de la Vega
Editor, Spanish: Rossana Zúñiga
Editor, English: Elizabeth Krajnik
Art Director: Michael Flynn
Book Design: Raúl Rodriguez
Illustrator: Aurora Aguilera

Cataloging-in-Publication Data

Names: Gregory, Martin.
Title: Stephen is a good grandson = Stephen es un buen nieto / Martin Gregory.
Description: New York : PowerKids Press, 2019. | Series: Doing our Part = Participemos | In English and Spanish. Includes index.
Identifiers: ISBN 9781538348383 (library bound)
Subjects: LCSH: Grandsons—Juvenile fiction. | Grandparents—Juvenile fiction. | Grandparent and child—Juvenile fiction.
Classification: LCC PZ7.G467 St 2019 | DDC [E]—dc23

CPSIA Compliance Information: Batch #CWPK19. For further information contact Rosen Publishing, New York, New York at 1-800-237-9932

Contenido

Contents

Stephen quiere mucho a sus abuelitos.
¡Le gusta visitarlos!

Stephen loves his grandparents!
He likes visiting them.

Nana y Papa son los padres de
la mamá de Stephen. Viven en el campo.

Nana and Papa are Stephen's mom's
parents. They live out in the country!

Cuando Stephen los visita, le gusta jugar afuera.

When Stephen visits them, he likes to play outside.

8

Juntos van de pesca y dan largos paseos.

They go fishing and take long walks.

9

Abuelita Marie es
la mamá del papá de Stephen.
Ella vive en la ciudad.

Gramma Marie is Stephen's dad's
mom. She lives in the city!

Cuando Stephen la visita, también dan paseos.

When Stephen visits her, they take walks, too.

Van a la panadería
y a la librería.

They go to the bakery
and the bookstore.

13

Stephen trata de ayudar a sus abuelitos.

Stephen tries to help his grandparents.

Él mismo recoge
sus cosas.

He picks up after himself.

15

Abuelita Marie le pide a Stephen
que la ayude a secar los platos.

Gramma Marie asks Stephen to help dry dishes.

Stephen rastrilla las hojas en casa de Nana y Papa.

Stephen rakes leaves at Nana and Papa's house.

Stephen tiene buenos modales.
Dice "por favor" y "gracias".

Stephen uses
his manners. He says "please"
and "thank you."

A Stephen le encanta escuchar los cuentos
de sus abuelos.

Stephen loves to listen to his grandparents' stories.

¡A veces son muy graciosos!

Sometimes they're very funny!

Stephen es
un buen nieto.
¡Sus abuelitos son
maravillosos!

22

Stephen is a good grandson.
His grandparents are
great grandparents!

Palabras que debes aprender
Words to Know

(la) panadería
bakery

(los) platos
dishes

pesca
fishing

Índice / Index